SESAME STREET

Elmo's CHRISTMAS COUNTDOWN

Adapted by Meg McLaughlin from the original screenplay by Joey Mazzarino
Illustrated by Tom Leigh

 Dalmatian Press, LLC, 2008. All rights reserved.
Published by Dalmatian Press, LLC, 2008. The DALMATIAN PRESS name and logo are trademarks of Dalmatian Press, LLC, Franklin, Tennessee 37067. No part of this book may be reproduced or copied in any form without written permission from the copyright owner.
Printed in the U.S.A.
ISBN: 1-40375-013-0 (X) 1-40375-571-1 (T)

08 09 10 NGS 7 6 5 4 3 2 1
17379 Sesame Street 8x8 Storybook: Elmo's Christmas Countdown

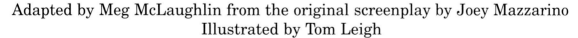

One day, when it was almost Christmas,
Elmo was whistling in the snow when…

...an elf fell out of Santa's sleigh and almost landed right on top of Elmo!

"Are you all right, little fellow?" the elf asked Elmo.
"Sorry about that rough landing."

"Elmo's fine, thank you. Who are you?"

"I'm the elf who helps Santa Claus find someone special to do the magical Christmas Countdown every year," answered the elf, brushing himself off. "It's done with this official Christmas Counter-Downer."

"Boy oh boy!" yelled Elmo. "Elmo has never met a real elf before! Um… what's the Christmas Counter-Downer?"

"It's a set of magical Christmas boxes," said the elf. "Christmas can't come without counting down the boxes from 10 to 1. But when my sleigh went *kablooey*, the official Counter-Downer boxes fell out and were lost," he sighed. "How will I ever find them so Christmas can come in time?"

"Elmo knows!" said Elmo. "Mr. Elf can make a wish on the Christmas star for a Christmas miracle!"

Little Elmo began wishing hard on a big, bright star. "Please let all the Counter-Downer boxes come back so Christmas can come again," he said. "Now you try, Mr. Elf."

"Wish on a Christmas star?" the elf said doubtfully. "Do you really think that will work, my furry red friend? The boxes will just appear out of nowhere?"

"Anybody lose a number 10?" asked Abby Cadabby—appearing out of nowhere.

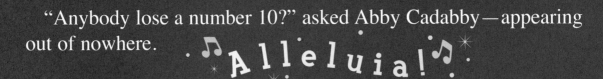

♪ Alleluia! ♪

"Oh, boy! It's Box Number 10—it's a Christmas miracle!" exclaimed Elmo. "See? Elmo told you, Mr. Elf. Abby has started the Christmas Countdown!"

The elf was confused. "Who are you?" he asked Abby.

"I'm Abby Cadabby, a fairy-in-training," Abby said, "and this box just bonked me on the wings."

"Oh, I see. Well, look, thank you, Miss Cadabby," the elf said, "but we are still missing nine boxes, and if we don't find them, Christmas is not coming. Why, just the thought of it makes me want to—"

YEOW!

"It's Bert!" cried Elmo. "What happened?"

"Well, I was eating my celebratory Christmas Eve oatmeal, when this box plopped into my bowl," Bert said.

"Box Number 9!" Abby shouted.

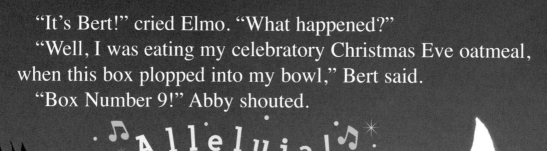

♪ Alleluia! ♪

"It's a miracle!" whooped Elmo.

"A miracle?" the elf echoed. "At this rate, the *next* box will just fall out of the sky!"

"Is Super Grover okay?" Elmo asked. "What happened?"

"I was just flying along, minding my own super business," said Super Grover, "when this adorable little box got caught in my cape."

"It's Box Number 8!" Abby exclaimed.

♪ Alleluia! ♪

"It's a Christmas miracle! Yay!" said Elmo.
"What's next!" wondered the elf. "I guess the next box will probably appear all wrapped and tied up with a bow!"

"Oh, hello!" said Big Bird, walking up with a pretty package. "Look
what I got you for Christmas, Elmo! I was just fluffing my feathers,
and it magically appeared!"

"Box Number 7," laughed Abby. "And it's wrapped with a nice little
bow, just like Mr. Elf guessed!"

"Sometimes you find just the perfect gift," smiled Big Bird.

♪♫ **Alleluia!** ♫♪

"Wow!" gasped Elmo. "You guessed exactly right, Mr. Elf. It's another Christmas miracle. And the nicest gift ever!"

"Miracles and magic are fine," grumbled the elf, "but we have boxes to find. This is serious work. It's not as easy as just pulling something out of a hat!"

"Hey, you guys, look what just popped out of my hat," chuckled Ernie. "Isn't it neat? *Hee-hee-hee…*"

"It's Box Number 6!" Abby squealed.

Allelu–

"Wait! Before you start singing, look closely," said the elf. "This is *not* Box Number 6. This is Box Number 5! And the boxes have be in order! 10, 9, 8, 7, 6, 5, 4, 3, 2, 1. This is a disaster! I've ruined Christmas."

"Don't worry," Elmo reassured the elf.
"Christmas just has to come," chimed in Abby. "We're sure to find Box Number 6 somewhere."

"As a matter of fact," said Ernie, "look what Rubber Duckie found in the bathtub. Ta-dah!"

"I knew it," shouted Abby. "It's Box Number 6!"

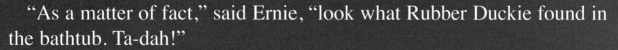

A l l e l u i a!

"It's another Christmas miracle! Yay!" said Elmo. "Now does Mr. Elf believe that everything will be okay?"

Suddenly…
"Look what I found in my bed!" said Papa Bear.
"Look what I found in my bed!" said Mama Bear.
"Take a gander at what I found in *my* bed," said Baby Bear.
"Whoa!" said Abby. "Boxes 4, 3, and 2!"

Alleluia!

"That's three Christmas miracles!" cheered Elmo.

Finally, the elf began to smile. "You know, I have a funny feeling I've never felt before—a feeling that the last box is going to just show up in some weird and unexpectedly strange way."

"It sounds like Mr. Elf believes in Christmas miracles!" said Elmo.

"I guess I do!" laughed the elf. "Ha-hah! I really do! I *do* believe in Christmas miracles! Whoa—oa!"

The elf was so excited that he jumped—slipped—and fell!

"Ouch! I've had a tumbly, stumbly day on Sesame Street! But wait … hey! I just landed on something small and hard. It couldn't be. It is! It's Box Number 1!"

"Oh, boy! Elmo thinks this is a real Christmas——"

"Wait! Let me say it! It's a real Christmas miracle!" proclaimed the elf.

♪ Alleluia! ♪

"10, 9, 8, 7, 6, 5, 4, 3, 2—and 1!" Elmo, Abby, and Mr. Elf chanted merrily as the last box was placed into the Counter-Downer. And from high overhead came a jolly "Ho-ho-ho!"

"It's a miracle," whispered Elmo.

"It's magical," added Abby.

"It's Christmas," said the elf.

Do you believe?